Roger McGough

The Lighthouse
that ran away

illustrated by Rosemary Woods

RED FOX

A Red Fox Book
Published by Random House Children's Books, 20 Vauxhall Bridge Road, London SW1V 2SA
A division of Random House UK Ltd., London, Melbourne, Sydney, Auckland, Johannesburg and agencies throughout the world
First published by The Bodley Head Children's Books 1991. Red Fox edition 1992. © Roger McGough 1991. Illustrations copyright © Rosemary Woods
The right of Roger McGough to be identitied as the author of this work has been asserted by him in accordance with the Copyright, Designs and Patents A
All rights reserved.   Printed in Hong Kong.   ISBN 0 09 997960 8

Breakneck Bay is a forlorn spot indeed. If you have ever been there (and I doubt if you have) then you will not have lingered. Rugged and unfriendly, Breakneck Bay is miles from anywhere, and likes it that way.

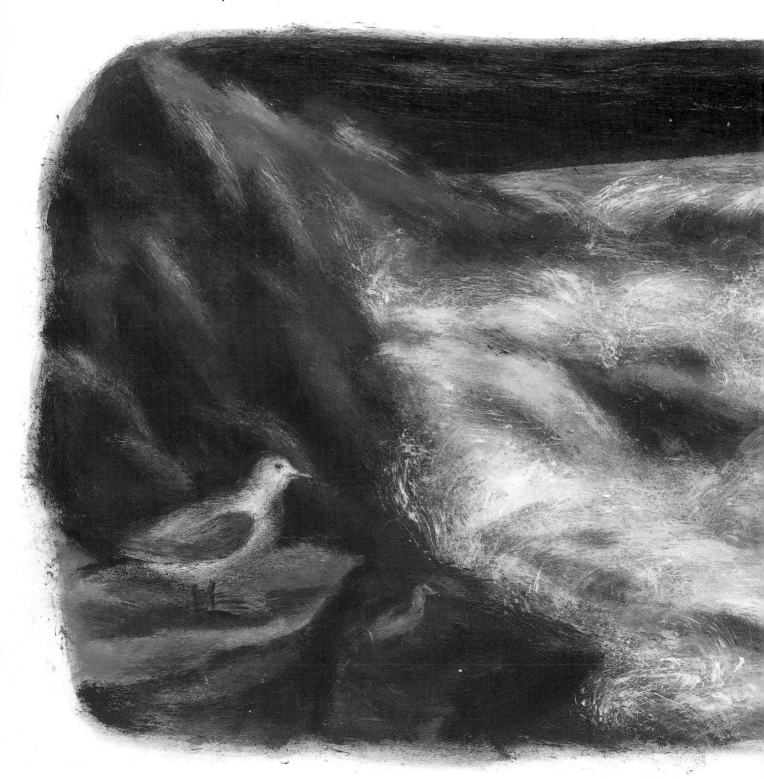

No pretty villages hug the coastline. No fishermen put out to sea. No hikers clamber over its cliffs. No children delve into its rocky pools. That part of the coast is dark and stormy all year round. For when winter takes its summer holiday, Breakneck Bay is where it goes.

And why is it called Breakneck Bay? Because years upon years ago, many a ship, blown off course and staggering blindly in the blackest of storms, had tripped over the rocks and been smashed to pieces.
It was a part of the coast that sailors feared and avoided at all costs:

"Never sail near Breakneck Bay
When the sun goes down – O
The devil waits for those who stray
And you will surely drown – O."

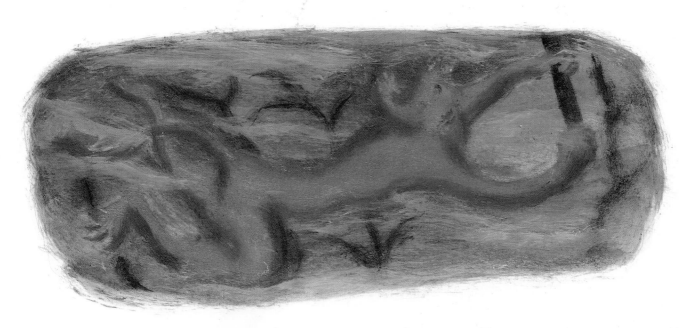

And so a lighthouse was built, with a powerful beam, that warned
ships to keep away from the mad rocks below.
Tall and proud it would sing:

> "Look out, steer clear
> Be guided by my light.
> Have faith, do not fear
> You shall not perish this night."

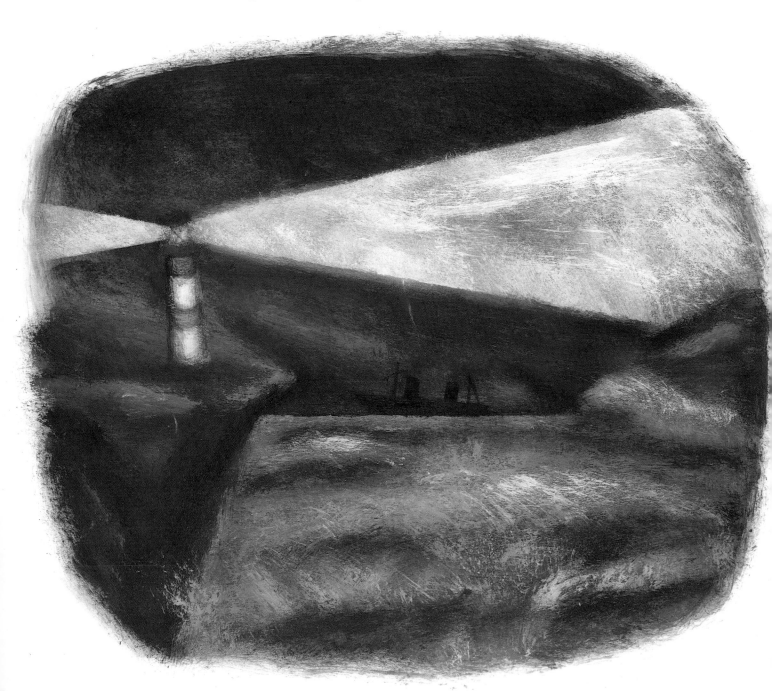

And sure enough, there were no more shipwrecks, and the sailors sang merrier shanties.

And then one day, not so very long ago, the lighthouse keeper turned off the lamp for the last time.
"Sorry old chum," he said, and talked about radar and about how nowadays ships were able to see in the dark.

"We're both too old now to be useful," he said, sadly, and gathering his few belongings, locked the door and left, never to return.

The lighthouse couldn't believe it. He'll come back soon, he thought, or another keeper will come. But no one did.

Years passed. The wild grass grew at his feet. His coat chipped and peeled, and his eyes dimmed. His hinges rusted and his shutters fell. He was so lonely. The only visitors were seagulls who came to perch and practise their screeching, and a few young rabbits who scampered around him each spring.

"What a sad and sorry sight
A lighthouse is without a light.

Abandoned cheerless and alone
A useless finger of painted stone."

Years passed. And whatever the weather, even on the rare sunny days, a grey cloud seemed to curl around him, so that he could see no further than his own unhappiness.

"What I'll do," thought the lighthouse,
when as down in the dumps as a lighthouse can be,
"What I'll do, is wait for a stormy night and then
jump off the cliffs into the sea. I will be dashed to pieces
against the rocks. Then they'll be sorry."

Who? The rocks? The lighthouse-keeper?
No. No one would be sorry.
He realised at last that nobody would come and
make things better.
If his life was to change then it was up to him.

The very next morning he ran away.
"The lighthouse guarding Breakneck Bay
was lonely, so one day
it simply upped and ran away."

To tell the truth, he didn't run very far. In fact, he didn't run at all, he tottered, or staggered, like a baby who has just learned to walk. His timbers were stiff and his joints rusty, but it was exciting nevertheless. The very fact of uprooting himself from the ground on which he had stood for over a hundred years – of turning his back on the horizon, at which he had gazed day and night – to leave the sea behind him forever, and stumble down the hill towards he knew not what, was scary but exciting. So exciting.

After a few shuffles he came to a halt – Out of breath already.

"This is no good," thought the lighthouse, "I don't know where I'm running away to, but wherever it is, it's going to take years at this rate."

Just then, a piece of wooden fencing, blown by the wind, rolled past. His brain sprung an idea. "That's the way to travel," he cried, and carefully and creakily, lay down on his side, and rocked himself until he began to roll.

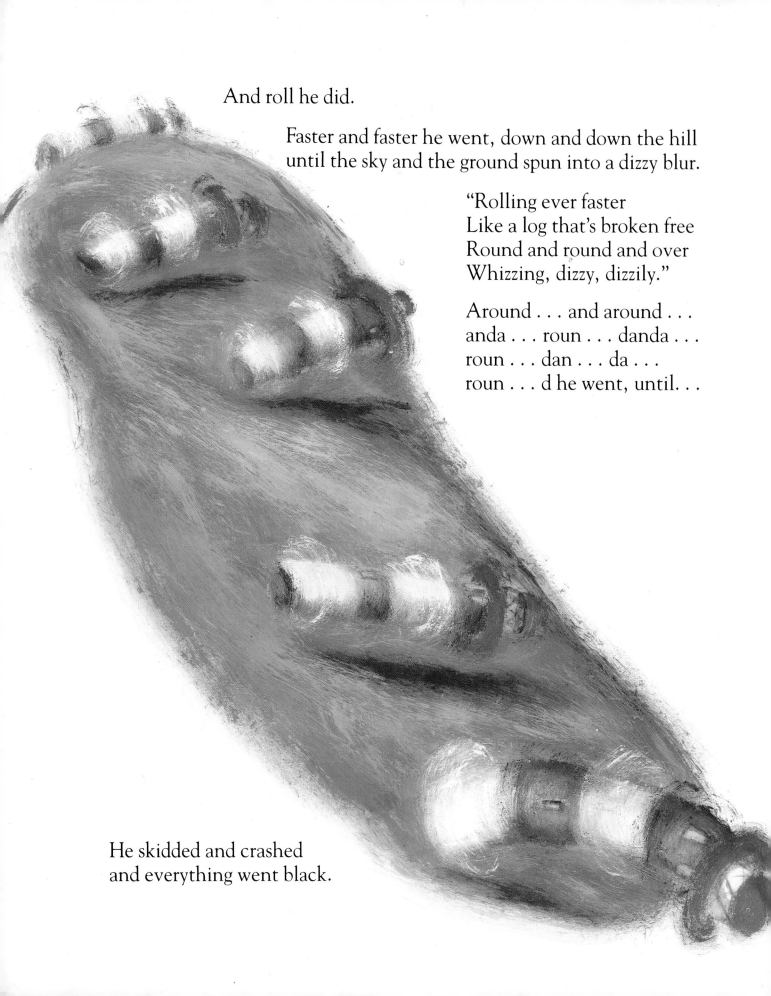

And roll he did.

Faster and faster he went, down and down the hill until the sky and the ground spun into a dizzy blur.

"Rolling ever faster
Like a log that's broken free
Round and round and over
Whizzing, dizzy, dizzily."

Around . . . and around . . .
anda . . . roun . . . danda . . .
roun . . . dan . . . da . . .
roun . . . d he went, until. . .

He skidded and crashed
and everything went black.

He awoke, giddy and bruised, but with nothing broken, to discover that he was lying across a railway line. A railway line? He thought about this for a few minutes until the sky was back in place (up there), and the ground was where it should be (down there), until the world had stopped revolving in fact.

And *then* he panicked.

Railway line means railway, and railway means Giant Monster with iron wheels that crushes and slices anything in its path.

The lighthouse rocked himself from side to side in an attempt to roll off the track. But try as he might he just couldn't manage to.

What's that whistle?
What whistle?
That train whistle. The whistle of a train. The crack-crack of wheels on a track. A train full of speed, full speed ahead, a head of steam, a scream of pain, a train clickety-clack over the track, crack-crack.

Roll and roll. Rock and roll. He rocked and rolled, he rocked and he rolled himself off the track. And just in time. For no sooner had he rolled clear of the railway lines than. . .

Nothing happened.
Nothing at all.
Well, to tell the truth,
a few birds flew over
and a frog cleared its throat . . .
but otherwise, nothing.
The lighthouse opened one eye
and then the other.
The sky was blue,
a few clouds strolled by,
hand in hand,
otherwise silence.
Pure, silken silence.

And then he heard it again, the whistle, the sound of a train. But this time he realised that the noise came not from the railway track but from over the embankment.

Curiosity killed the cat, but as far as we know it never killed a lighthouse. Cautiously he squirmed his way, lighthouse-fashion, up to the ridge, and peered over and saw. . .

Spread out before him with all the fun of the fair – a fun fair! His eyes
lit up at the magic of it all. In all his life he had never seen such excitement,
such movement, such jingle jangle:

Ferris wheel and roller-coaster, carousels and dodgem cars,
coconut shies and hoop-la stalls, strong men and tattooed ladies,
and a train. . . A ghost train!

With each new colour, sound and smell his eyes widened and shone so brightly that people began to notice him, and point and marvel. Even Henry J. Fingle himself (for it was Fingle's Fun Fair) left his caravan to see what the commotion was about.

And there was the centre of attention, a lighthouse,
towering above everything, sending its golden beams in all directions.

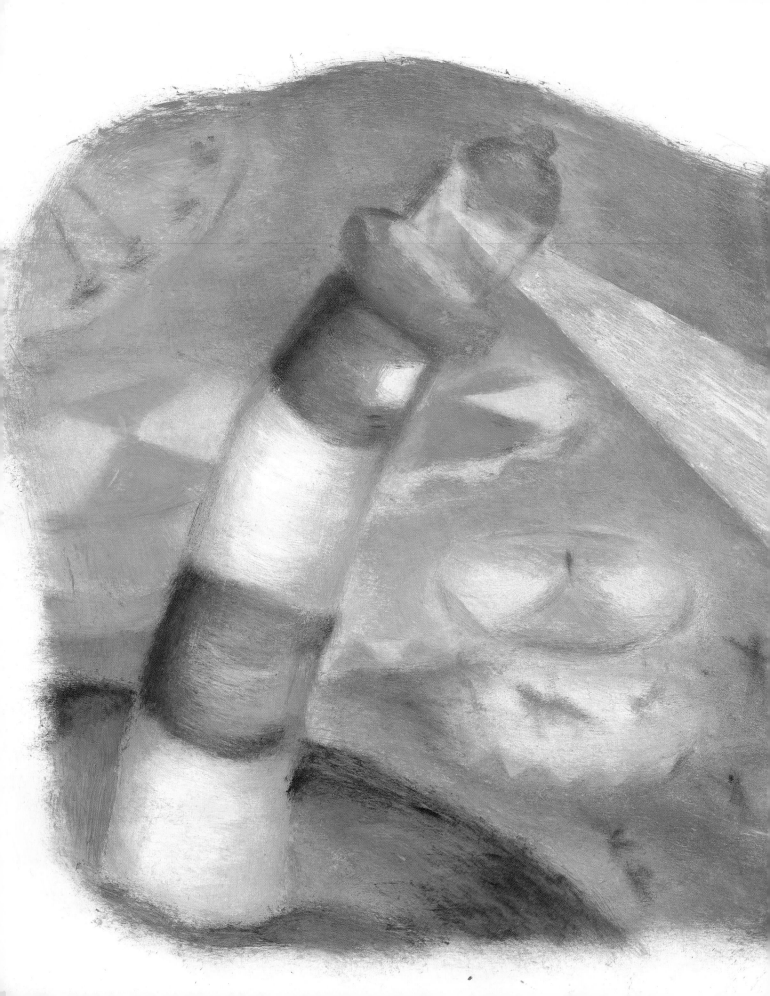

"What an attraction!" cried Henry J., "That's just what the fun fair needs," and climbed straight up to the lighthouse, introduced himself and made an offer.

And that's how the lighthouse came to join a travelling fun fair.
Of course he's not a lighthouse anymore.

The carpenters and the painters got to work and turned him overnight into the handsomest helterskelter that ever there was.

He travels all over the world now.

And it's no longer the seagulls screeching that he hears,
or the wind moaning, but the laughter and excited squeals of the children
as they slide around him, time after time, dizzy with delight.